Prisoners

Books by Jerome Gold

The Negligence of Death
Of Great Spaces (with Les Galloway)
The Inquisitor
Life at the End of Time (chapbook)
The Prisoner's Son
Prisoners
Hurricanes (editor)
Publishing Lives: Interviews with Independent Book
Publishers in the Pacific Northwest
and British Columbia

Prisoners

Jerome Gold

Black Heron Press
Post Office Box 95676
Seattle, Washington 98145
http://mav.net/blackheron

Some pieces in this book originally appeared in the following publications: *Emerald City Comix, Chiron Review, clear-cut: anthology, Friday's Egg Calendar, Poets on the Line, War Stories* (chapbook) and *Life at the End of Time* (chapbook).

Published by Black Heron Press
          Post Office Box 95676
          Seattle, Washington 98145
          http://mav.net/blackheron

Contents

Prisoners

inspired by the experience
of Lê Huu Trí

At the end of three months they told us we
had worked well on the farm. We had met
our quotas, planting the right number of
cassava trees, weeding the expected number
of hectares, cutting wood sufficient to construct
new houses for the cadre. We had obeyed the
guards and fewer prisoners were feigning
illness. One prisoner had escaped but he had
been caught and shot, his body returned.
Beginning tomorrow our morning work
break would be extended to half an hour and
we would be permitted twenty minutes
to bathe in the river.

           They read to us from the newspaper:
anti-government demonstrations in the south;
our ancient enemies attacking us once again
in the north; terrorist bombings in the cities.

           None of us believed anything.
We thought only about the food we would
eat that day.

In The Machine

War Years

On the morning the Japanese bombed Pearl
Harbor, my father was racing Adolphe Menjou
across the Arizona desert to California.
Adolphe Menjou was driving a yellow roadster.
Both men were having the time of their lives.

Six months later, driving east across Texas,
my father was chased by a tornado following
Route 66. Outside a town a Mexican woman
with thirteen children, or maybe seven, ran
out onto the highway, forcing my father to
veer wildly to avoid driving into her or her
children. My father did not stop. The tornado
blackened the town on either side of the road
behind him and then it took the woman and
her children.
When my father told the story of the
tornado and the woman and her children he
did not emphasize but did acknowledge her
differentness from him, from him and me.
And anyway, if he had stopped, he could not
have saved her and her children, not all of
them. And who would decide which of them
would not fit in the car? Anyway there was
no time, not even to stop for one—one child,
or the woman alone, perhaps. What did I

expect from him? Should he have died with
them to show solidarity?

Many years later, driving east again, but through
New Mexico, my father was once more pursued
by a tornado. In the car with him were my
mother, my sister, and me. This time, the
tornado gaining on us (he said when he
recounted the story to my uncles and their
wives) but still a mile or two behind, he
stopped and turned the car and drove back
west into the twister as fast as he could get the
car to go. It was a 1946 Lincoln Cosmopolitan
and it weighed more than two tons. It had a
V12 engine and it went unswervingly if with
some hesitation directly into and through the
storm. Afterward sand was pitted into the fenders
of the car an eighth of an inch and the
windshield had to be replaced.
When my father told this story he did not
say that other cars with smaller engines had not
turned but had outrun the twister. We met
some of their passengers at a cafe when our
new windshield was being placed. My father
risked the lives of his wife, his daughter, his
son, himself. For what?

*

My father loved speed, hated moral quandaries.
And, given the occasion and a reasonable
chance to survive, he loved the violence
of embracing his enemy whom he loved more
than my mother, my sister, me. Though, to be
accurate, when he and Adolphe Menjou heard on
their respective radios the news about Pearl
Harbor, both men slowed their cars.

The Builder

They would lure the dogs with chunks of bloody
meat, then grab them from behind and cut their
throats when they went for it. Shepherds, they
were always shepherds. He hated those dogs.
Then they would crawl into the camps of the
sleeping Germans and cut their throats too.

He left Warsaw after his brother was killed, the
last member of his family. After Warsaw, he told
someone, he was always alone. "In here," he
said, hammering his fist against his chest, "is ice."
The first partisans he met were Poles, and Poles
being what they are, they tried to give him to
the Germans in exchange for—who knows what.
He left one dead and a second he thought with
luck would die. Whose luck he did not say.
Finally he found partisans who were Jews. It
was then he learned how to kill Germans by
killing their dogs first. When the Russians
came he was sixteen.

In San Francisco he built buildings. He had a talent
for organizing men to do what he wanted them
to do. He hired them for work and dropped them in
times of scarcity. In that he was no different
from others in his trade. His competitors

were targets for whatever he could devise.
Once he followed one home, a man entirely
unaware, a man convinced that life is
something other than what it is. That time
he did nothing, did not even poison the man's
dog, a shepherd. But another time he used fire.

His forearms were gnarled as cancers on the
boles of trees, his hands thick as clubs. He
contemned everything that breathed but the wife
he had met in a DP camp. They had no
children—she was not able, her Fallopian tubes
having been cemented, then removed.
In any event he had no desire to bring
life into a dead world. He knew what was
important. What was important was to bring
destruction upon everyone you did not love.

How the Lieutenant Was Saved

This story was told to me.

The platoon was about to go into a village when the lieutenant joined them. He had been in-country for five days. That afternoon they captured a North Vietnamese soldier. When they laagered for the night the lieutenant radioed his commander for a helicopter to evacuate the prisoner.

It will be dark soon, his commander said. He doubted that a pilot would be willing to fly at night to pick up a prisoner.

The lieutenant said his situation was too insecure to keep the prisoner with him.

His commander agreed with the lieutenant's assessment.

"Well, what should I do, sir?"

His commander did not reply.

"What do you want me to do, sir?"

Again there was no reply. The lieutenant felt emptiness engulf him, drawing something out of him so that he felt the emptiness inside himself as well as without.

He set down the radio. He was crying. He walked over to where the prisoner lay tied up and aimed his rifle at him. He caught his breath and pressed the trigger. The rifle did not fire and he realized he had forgotten to release the safety. But he heard then from left and right the shrill, ear-piercing clap of the platoon's M16s discharging in unison.

The lieutenant knew suddenly that in causing him to forget to release the safety, and in moving his platoon up beside him, and having them fire the killing shots, Jesus Christ had performed a miracle on his behalf, for the prisoner was dead and the lieutenant was blameless.

And this is how the lieutenant was saved.

The Motorcyclist

Buff called about six.
She would be staying late.
A motorcyclist had broken his head
and they were trying to put it back
together. I was disappointed
but I didn't press her.

At dusk the smog condensed into
gray and brown strata outside the
window. It descended like a sheath
over the buildings, enveloping
most of the hospital across the street.
At eight I ate without appetite.

Louise refilled my cup. "Something
must be going on. One of
the nurses called and said Rob wouldn't
be finished till around ten." She
moved on to the next booth to pour
coffee for the docs sitting there. Buff
had had something with her husband
and it had ended only a couple
of months ago. What was strange was that
Louise and I now looked at each
other with suspicion while Buff and Rob
got along famously.

*

"Kirshner says they're in surgery."
Louise poured herself a cup of coffee
and sat down across from me. "I
just can't trust him anymore." She had
waitressed for six years to put Rob through
medical school and internship.
Now it looked like she was going to be
cheated of the dividends. Rob
was sleeping with a nurse.

"You could dump him," I said.
        "Don't think I haven't thought about it."

"Let me take you away from all this."
        "Why couldn't you have asked a year
ago? Even six months? Now I'm
too tired," Louise said.

"And you don't like me."
        "I don't trust you," she corrected.
"How could you have let her
do it? Doesn't it do anything
to you inside?"

"I didn't have much choice in the
matter," I said. "Come on. Let's go in

the bar. I'll buy you a drink."
      "And then?"

"I'll take you home."
      "The last thing I need is a mercy fuck."

Around ten the wind came up and blew
the smog out to sea. It was
going to be a santa ana, you could
see it in the way the palm trees bent.
Louise put on her jacket and got
her handbag from behind the counter. "I
couldn't reach Rob. Would you tell
him I've gone home? I'm
off Wednesday. Call me?"

I promised I would.

Buff and Rob
came in together an hour later.
They looked as though half of themselves
had evaporated.
"Louise went home," I said.
Rob started to sit down next to
Buff opposite me but changed his mind.
"I'll see you tomorrow," he told her.

*

"I have to relax for a minute
before we go home," Buff said. The
moisture in her eyes surprised me.
        "Do you want a drink?"

"I just want to rest for a minute."
        "How was it?"

"He died."
        "Are you going to take him
home with you?"

"No. He's dead. I can't do anything
more. I'm ready now." She slid
across the seat and stood up. "How
was your day?"

"This one's different, isn't it?" I
said when we were on the freeway.
        "He was so polite. Even when the
receptionist asked all those stupid
questions. He called all of the
doctors sir and the nurses ma'am and
he was so grateful when Hanks gave him
a sip of water."

*

"What did he call you?" I asked.
        "Ma'am. I didn't want to confuse him."

After a while she said, "When we
took his helmet off his head just
fell apart. It wouldn't have been
so bad if he just hadn't
been so polite."

The First Dead Man I Ever Saw

When I saw my first dead man
I was walking home from school.
It was late winter, the beginning
of spring. Leaves were green but sparse.
The road I followed took me
along the flank of a hill.
At the bottom the dead man lay.

Two men were walking away
from him, starting up toward the road.
I was certain the man was dead,
don't ask me how I knew.
Maybe because he was so flat,
as though constructed in
two dimensions. His raised knee
fell to the side. It was his left
knee. I saw everything clearly.
It was autumn, actually,
and the leaves were sparse and brown.

The two men were climbing the hill.
They were looking at their feet.
I saw them. I continued walking,
looking back once. They had reached the
road and were walking away from me.

18

*

At home I turned the television
on and off. I poured milk into
the sink, emptied the dog's dish into
the garbage bag. When my parents arrived
I told them what I had seen.
They called the sheriff's office and
a deputy came over.
I told him what I saw.
Don't tell anybody else, he said.
Then he went away.

Yes, he told my parents when
he came back, the man is
where your son said he was,
and he is dead.
Then the deputy said, It's
very important that your son
not say anything more. Nor should you.

We didn't. Not even to each other.
I didn't.

I saw a dead man and the
men who killed him. I never
learned who he was, nor who they
were, nor why they killed him.

Money and Its Loss

...My job
is to love all that happens.
—Larry Laurence

I was fired after one night. The day crew was angry—I had left them to do what I had been unable to do. The owner did not want to pay me, wadding up a $10 bill and throwing it on the floor. I bent to pick it up because it was $10 and I had nothing. It had been a dishwashing job.

I stank unbearably of decaying food. At our studio flat I lay down on the sofa so quietly I might have been in another country. But my wife woke, wanting to know why I was sleeping on the sofa. "I stink. And I'm too tired to shower." "What's really wrong?" she asked. I told her and she said "Come to bed" and I went and closed the warm smell of her girl body over me. She was 17, I a year older, almost to the day.

It wasn't the first job I'd been fired from. The first was a warehouseman's job, spending each day stacking 106-lb. bags of white trinity in boxcars. I weighed 165 lbs.; it took me 3 weeks to bulk up, my forearms to swell and my shoulders to thicken and my hands to harden and crack and bleed and finally to become numb to pain but unable to grasp a cup by its handle. Once, having stacked

every one of a pallet of bags, I grabbed the man
beside me by neck and crotch and threw him on top
of the last bag. Motion was everything, motion and
rhythm. Forget thinking.

It took my body 3 weeks to get to that
point but it was too late. By the 15th day the foreman
had decided to let me go after my 30-day probation.
Sorry, he said. Yes, you can do the job. Yes, I decided
too soon. But it's too late. The hardest thing about
going away from that job was the loss of the money
that had seemed so sure, that had allowed us to
marry. But that was how it was going to be: money
and its loss, love and its betrayal.

I'm Frank

Yeah. I'm Frank. I placed a nuclear device on the bottom of a certain harbor in Southeast Asia. Yeah. Set to be triggered by satellite. This was during the war in that part of the world. That was what my team did, set nuclear devices. We did other things, too. Then I got out of the Navy. Could not tolerate civilian life. Could not do it.

So I went into smuggling. Good money, good excitement. I was good at it. Oh, yeah—when I was still in the Navy I smuggled M16s to Marcos from Viet Nam. This was for the CIA. It was their op. I was on loan.

Anyway, after the war I went into smuggling. Marijuana. Cocaine. Mexico. South America. Built landing strips in Texas, Oklahoma. I had a talent for organization. An eye for detail. I got caught, spent two years in a federal prison. US federal, not Mexican federal.

Now I've been out for a while. I'm trying to get my life in order. I am getting my life in order. I don't do drugs anymore. Don't sell them, don't use them. I drink. Sometimes. Usually not. But sometimes. Christ.

My wife left me. Took the kids, two little girls. Tough, yeah. They'll end up hating me. I'm working at getting them back. Meanwhile, I'm living with this woman who does a lot for me. Helps me with the paperwork for the VA. I cannot tolerate paperwork.

I'm bipolar. Manic-depressive. Up and down. That's what the Navy did—took a bunch of manic-y kids and trained us to plant nuclear devices. And do other things. They were looking for a certain personality type. I'm it. I admit, though, I liked it.

I go to the VA, I want to talk about placing a nuclear device in a certain harbor of a certain country in Southeast Asia, and the psychiatrist says, "Sorry. We can't talk about that." But that's what I've got to talk about. "Sorry, we can't talk about that."

I had a stroke last year. Then something in my gut burst. I recovered, but it made me think. I don't want to live here anymore. I don't want to live in the United States. It's too cold for me here. So I'm going to go down to Mexico with my girlfriend. Maybe we'll be back in the spring. Fuck America.

The Banality of Evil

Thirty something, forty something—how can
you tell nowadays, so attractive, so
spare in that raw corporate way
are these assistant professors
—she is bitter about the
hurdles she must jump in order to
advance her career. "Sometimes you have to
do things you don't want to do," she complains.

We are in the garden behind her
chairman's house. Roses, trellis-bound, send
a heavy, tropical scent into
the moist air, excite a faint
sexuality. One of us, a
friend of the chairman's nephew,
asks if she would send blacks to
concentration camps if her dean told her
to. He asks in search of a limit,
a boundary she will not cross.
It is conversation. We are
discussing abstractions. Soon we will
go inside for dinner.

"Sometimes you have to do things you don't
want to do," she says again.

How I Became a Robber and a Killer

This is how I became a robber. I was going to go to the ATM. I had actually started out the door, but then I remembered how I'd been robbed by a guy with a gun at an ATM. Not the last time I was there, no, a long time ago. He'd been waiting for someone. It could have been anyone, but it was me. He made me empty my account—I think I had about a hundred and fifty dollars—and I handed it over to him because he had a gun.

So this time—actually, I was already in the car, driving to the ATM, when I remembered how I'd been robbed. And I turned around and went back to my place and got my gun, and then I went to the ATM. And I was waiting in the line—there were four or five people ahead of me—and I had my hands in my pockets because I was cold, and my right hand was on the butt of my piece and I figured, why not? Why not? So I did. I got those people—by this time there were only three of them—and one by one I had them empty their accounts, or nearly. I let them each keep a couple of dollars. I didn't want to have it on my conscience that I let anyone starve. You know? So that's how I became a robber.

This is how I shot a guy. I went to this ATM I'd checked out earlier, and I was waiting there in a car—no, not mine, one I'd stole—and I was across the street and I see this guy walking up to the ATM, and you know who it is? It's the guy who robbed me. Who I told you about. At least I think it is. It looked like him. I didn't get a real good look at him when he robbed me because I was looking at the gun. You know? His hand on the gun. Looking to see if he was going to shoot me. I was pretty sure he was the same guy. I mean I didn't have any doubts. What I was going to do was go up to him and scare the shit out of him like he did me, and maybe rob him. But when he turned around—because he'd heard me, see? I was running across the street at him. Or maybe he saw me out of the corner of his eye. I think I yelled something at him, I don't remember what—I shot him. I emptied my piece in him. It was revenge, for robbing me. So that's how I killed someone. If I had known I was going to kill someone I wouldn't have bothered to steal a car.

How It Can Happen

It can happen like this: you're
driving and a car on your right
has a yield sign—or a
stop. And instead of yielding
or stopping, the driver
accelerates because
maybe he got confused,
maybe he has Alzheimer's
like that president, or
maybe his foot got twisted
under the pedal—who knows?
All we know is that he
hit the gas instead of
the brake. It can happen
like that. It probably has.

Or suppose you're driving
at night and you come around
this bend and there's this tractor-
trailer coming with his high
beams on and you don't even
see the pole you hit. That
happened.

It could happen in war. You
could be a prisoner, you

could have just been taken
prisoner, and they're hoisting you
up to their helicopter
through the trees and you get caught,
tangled or something, but they
don't stop, they just keep trying
and trying to pull you up
through the branches. That
happened. The man who told it
said, "All we got finally
was some bloody shorts." And said again,
"All we got was some bloody shorts."

A volcano could do it. You
could be drowned by mud or burned
by lava until your bones
were bare. Even in your sleep.
You might not even know.

You could starve.

You could fall in a bad winter
and freeze to your basement floor.
That happened.

Army ants could get you.

A shark, as you swam. You
could fall overboard while fishing
alone. You could be abducted
and tossed into an empty field.

Somebody could shoot you
as you walked on
the sidewalk. Or sat on your
porch. Or made love.

All of these ways and they
are none of them accidents. We
always know why they happen
after they happen.
Non-accidents, occurring
without warning or reason,
like life.

Who's Going to Kill Me

It's a windy day, a rain storm blowing
up from the south, everything clean and fresh.
I'm at a corner waiting to cross
when one of those cars with a metallic
finish and dark windows throbbing with rap
that you know is filled with little gangsta
mothahfuckahs stops in the crosswalk just as
the light turns. This broad, 35, 40,
business type, professor maybe, lawyer,
briefcase, power suit, goes up, kicks the
door. Immediately the window comes
down you see her yammering
   "the music this"
   "the crosswalk that"
   "inconsideration of the other"
       then

she walks on, grinning, you can see
she can hardly wait to tell her colleagues,
lawyers, professors, whatevers, how
she put these punks in their place.
But of course what she doesn't see is
these four little punks get out of the car
taking their little
   .22's
   9 em em's
   .38's

out of their pants, my saying "Hey, man, let
'er go, she's my sister, she's crazy, she
don't know what she's doin' half the time,
hell all the time," praying they're looking
for an excuse not to kill her, not to
thread that phony ringletted yellow hair
through her skull and knot it across
her little self-satisfied mouth.
They say "Yeah, keep your crazy sister
at home. Next time don't matter she's crazy."

But it's not over. A week later, a
dirty yellow day, the sun like
a lead weight pulling the sky down,
I'm at a party, a little soiree,
professional types except for me
but I'm with my girl friend, and
there's this broad, she's telling these other
professional types how she put these
little assholes down, that's all they need,
is to be shown their place, shown who's what.
I go over, say "Yeah, I heard about it."
She looks at me like who the fuck am I,
she says "How could you have heard about
it, I only told a couple people?" I say
"Actually, I was there." She looks at me.

I say "Actually, you almost got your
dumb ass shot and if I or someone hadn't
convinced those kids not to fuck you up
you would be dead right now and this kind
of fucking stupid-ass boasting I hear
coming out of your mouth turns my
stomach because I can just see someone—
maybe me—getting his ass killed
because of something you do, dig?"
There is quiet while everybody including
my girl friend stares at me like I got
shit on my shoes, they just now figured
out where the smell is coming from.
Then she says "No, really, where did you
hear about it? Did so and so tell you?"

When I was in Viet Nam I knew that
when I got killed it would be because
some clerk in some office who never
heard of me fucked up. Misfiled something,
mistyped something. Something. And that's
who this broad is. She's the clerk in the office in
the city I never been to who's going to kill me.

Ritual

He had already started to sweat when he woke up. Somebody was in the house. Or the tree limb was rubbing against the outside. The wind. Somebody was in the house.

He slipped out from under the blankets. His wife was still asleep. He found the Ruger under the bed. He pulled back the hammer with his thumb until he heard a soft click. The gun was on safety now but needed only a fraction of an inch more pull to cock the hammer to fire.

The sweat was drying. He was growing cold. He was naked. He considered putting on some clothes but that would take time.

The bedroom door was warped. It stuck. It always did. He pulled. The door sprang away from the frame, making a heavy tearing sound.

His wife opened her eyes. "What are you doing? Oh, come back to bed, Paul."

"I'll be back in a minute," he said quietly. He stepped outside the room, closing the door behind him, though not all the way.

First the kids' rooms. All right. Nobody in Leah's room. Now the boys'. All right. He moved to the stairs. He took one step down and stopped. He listened. The wind was up. It was probably the wind he had heard. Maybe it was blowing the tree limb. He went down two more stairs. Stopped. Listened. Two more. The next one will creak; stretch past it. Wait. Wait.

He crouched. He was shivering but had begun to sweat again. It smelled like acid. It might be the wind. It probably was. That time outside of Duc Co, he was caught in the ravine. One of them above, the other coming in after him. Get one, the other gets you. First one moved. One step. Then the other. One step. Night and shadows. One step. Then another.

The harsh acid smell came from him freely. He was practically swimming in it. He was shaking. If there were two he would shoot one, roll, come up and pop the other. Remember to keep one eye shut for the muzzle flash.

He was at the last stair. He stepped down, crouched, listened. Light poured in through the living room windows. It was white and lustrous, reflected off the snow. It was cold and death. He stank.

He duckwalked into the living room, squatted, his back against the wall by the heating vent. Catch them against the light. Kill them. Kill them. Kill them.

He listened.

Eventually he stood up. Took a breath. Fuck it.

He went upstairs.

Too tired to shower, he washed his armpits, then went to bed. He hoped he would sweat. If he could sweat that good clean nightsweat he would feel right in the morning.

In The Facility

What I Saw

Here's what I saw:
This Mexican and this black guy
were fighting in an alley.
The black guy was getting
the best of the Mexican
and the Mexican pulled out
a knife and stabbed the black. Then
the Mexican cut the black guy
here and around here and peeled
the skin off his face. You see that
when you're three or four years old,
it leaves an impression.
You know?

When I was little there'd
be dead guys in our flower
bed in the morning when I woke
up. It didn't seem funny
then like it is now when you
think of dead guys and flowers.
Gang stuff, yeah.
Then when I got bigger I'd
find my homies dead. I miss
them all the time, even if
they are still in my mind.

*

I think about it all the time,
you know? I dream about
it, I fantasize about
doing it. Violence. I love
it more than anything. More
even than females. I've shot a lot
of enemies, though
I haven't, as far as I know,
killed any. Though maybe I have.
If I die? So what. I'll be
with my homies in Heaven
or Hell, it makes no difference.
And if there's nothing, I won't care.

Oh yeah, one more thing I saw:
my dad after he blew his
brains out. He'd been in
Viet Nam. I guess he
couldn't take it anymore. That's
what everybody said.
Whatever "it" was.

Document: Take It

Take it.
Take it.
Bitch.
(When I got to the party the first thing
I saw was blood slipping
out from under the bathroom door.)

Where that broom? Take that broom.
(Grace was doing it. Naw,
I don't know why.)

You like that broom? Be still or I hurt you
worse again.
(Yeh, I know why. This girl had, you know,
she done it with the father of Grace's baby.
That what Grace said.
Maybe it's true she done it.
It probably is.)

Who next? My arm tired. Give her somethin' real.
I want to watch somebody on her.
(She came with two other bitches,
but they was allowed to go home after they
slapped them up a little.
Not me.

I wasn't there yet.
Grace. Maybe some of the others
who were there before me.
I don't know.
Somebody said these bitches thought
they was coming to a party.
They were invited to come to a party.)

Who next? Where that dog? What you laughin'
at? You ain't done nothin' yet!
(Yeh, I saw her.
It was bad.
She couldn't see, you know? Her eyes was shut.
Swole. She couldn't open them.
So she didn't know who was doing
what to her.
Yeh, she know Grace
because Grace was the one who beat on her first.
Her eyes wasn't swole yet
when Grace was first hitting her.)

Where that dog? Get me some o' that dog
shit out in the yard.
(Yeh, my brother pimped her.
Miko, yeh, we got the same daddy.
Maybe that is why. That could be part of the reason

why they did it.
She didn't want to work for Miko no more.
He told me.
No, Miko wasn't the father of Grace's baby.
Marcus was.)

Take it.
Take that.
Bitch. Bitch.
(I don't think Miko told Grace to do nothin'.
Why would he have to?
He could of beat her down hisself if he wanted to.
Yeh, he was there. Naw, he didn't rape her.
She wasn't nothin' to him by the time it come
to people rapin' her.)

We let her rest now. Let her sleep.
She bleed to death,
we keep at her without letting her rest.
(Marcus is dead. Somebody killed him. After, yeh.)

Wake up, bitch. You sleep long enough.
You got more company.
(She would of died, the police didn't come.
She couldn't even walk no more.
I was there two days

and they started on her before I come.
Two days.
Not all the time.
I'd go out, you know.
Come back.
Get something to eat.
Come back.
I know she identified me. But she couldn't see,
so she couldn't identify me.
She said she heard me laughing, yeh.
But I wasn't one of the people rapin' her.
I was there though. Yeh.
I don't know why I was laughing.
Wasn't nothing funny.)

Take it.
Take it.
This gonna go on forever.
This gonna go on after you dead.
(Yeh, Grace got sentenced
as an adult. Nine years.
She the only one.
But now me,
they say they're going to try me as an adult. Naw,
a different charge.
I killed a baby.
I was after its mama.)

This Is About a Murder

It began—we went to a dance.
One of my homies said something
to this girl and she, you know,
she said something too. She was laughing.
We didn't know she was with
this other—these other boys.
And one of them called my friend a nigger.
And he came over to us
and he told us that this Mexican
called him a nigger.
And I got hot. I don't know why.
And I wanted to get them,
the Mexican guys. We could see them
grouping up and talking just like
we were doing, so we knew
something was going to happen.

They left first. Then we did.
We walked out into the parking lot.
My homie who was talking with the girl
walked ahead. He was in front of us
maybe fifty or seventy-five feet. And
they were waiting by their car. And
they shot him—pop pop pop—a .22.
In the shoulder.
Then they took off in their car

and we got in our car
and followed them to a park
about a block from this elementary school where
they stopped.
And we stopped.

They must not have figured that
we had guns too, probably
because we didn't shoot back when
they shot at us—shot my homie.
But that was because our guns were in
the car. They were stupid.
They only had the double deuce. We had
two tray-eights and a 12-gauge shotgun.
We shot them all, but one.
We shot at him but he was lucky.
There were a couple of girls—the one
and then another.
The one boy we shot in the front with the 12-gauge
recovered fully.
I'm just joking.
The others were just shot
in the arm
in the shoulder
in the leg.

*

I don't know what we could have done different.
Maybe not done anything
when they called my homie a nigger.
But when we were putting the guns in the car
before we went to the dance
we talked about killing somebody that night.
I knew I was going to kill somebody that night.

A Life in Parts

1.

One time my stepfather told me to go into his bedroom and get his gun. He said he was going to shoot my mother. We were at the dinner table, all of us—him and my mother and my sister and me. I didn't say anything, I just didn't do it. So he told me again and this time I told him no. Then he went into the bedroom and came out with the gun and I got up and hit him in the face. He pistol-whipped me with that gun. It was the worst beating I ever took. But he didn't shoot my mother.

2.

We'd bought a couple of forties and were sitting in the car drinking them, you know, feeling good, relaxed, letting the stress go. We'd been huffing gas, too, so everything was kind of silly. We were parked under a light. I remember that. That made it easier for them. They just stopped right next to us, a guy stuck an Uzi out of the window and hosed our car. I remember when I saw the Uzi I thought—or maybe I said—"Uh oh." We were so drunk and so high we couldn't move. They hosed the car and I just sat there. And then they left. I checked myself over and I wasn't shot. I couldn't believe it. I started laughing. I turned to my homie—I was going to say how weird or lucky or something this was, they sprayed the whole damn car and didn't hit us—and I saw the blood coming out of his temple.

He was the homie I was closest to. My best friend. It's hard for me to believe that he went to Hell. But we did some bad things together, so I guess he's there, and I guess I'll see him there. We'll have fun.

3.

Once my homie and me were walking on the sidewalk—I was carrying my bat. I used to carry a bat because that was legal. You could get in trouble if a cop stopped you and you were carrying a gun. I was feeling really drugged out, you know? We'd huffed gas the night before and I was feeling...I don't know what I was feeling. And I saw this car with just the driver cruise by, and I knew he would go around the block and come back. I knew the car. I knew it belonged to someone in another...clique, I guess you'd call it.

So he came around again and stopped and got out of the car, and he was strapped. He had this .22 which, even though it's not a .357 or a nine em-em, will still kill you very nicely. He pointed it at me and he said he was going to shoot me. And I started walking toward him. Go on, I told him. Shoot. I don't give a shit. Go on.

But he didn't do it. Obviously. I could see his hand shaking. I don't know what he expected me to do—beg him for my life, maybe. I kept telling him, Go on. Do it. Calling him a coward. In Spanish, because he was a Mexican. But he didn't. He tried to back away but by then I was close and I hit him with the bat. Man, I did a job on him with that bat. My homie had to stop me so he could get the gun.

I don't know why I wasn't afraid. Maybe because I was so hung over. It would have been the same to me if he killed me or if he didn't. I learned one thing though. If you're ready to die, then you can kill. I don't know if the opposite is true, that if you're not ready to die, then you can't kill. Nah, you can kill someone under any circumstances. But it's easier if you want to die too.

4.

That .22 was a good gun because I had all this ammunition for it from a burglary I'd done a few days before. So I had that gun and I saw this car drive up outside of my apartment. I recognized the car as from the same clique that guy was from that we beat up, so just as they were getting out I started shooting into it. There were six or seven of them and they ran everywhere, and I just kept shooting into the car. I must have reloaded—I don't know how many times I reloaded. That was the most fun I ever had in my life.

The reason the police came was because I was shooting into the lot across the street. This was after the car. That night. I knew where these guys lived. They lived on the other side of that lot in some apartments a block away. Actually, I was shooting at those apartments but the police thought I was shooting into the empty lot. When I saw them pull up I hid the gun in a hole in my mattress. I was surprised they didn't find it. They asked about all the .22 shells on my floor but I said I didn't know anything about it because I'd just come home. Then they found a .32 I'd gotten in a burglary and put in my closet and forgot about, and first they got me on possession of a stolen firearm and then they changed it to Burg One.

5.

I was coming back from somewhere—I think I'd gone somewhere on a buy. We pulled into my street and—we couldn't. It was blocked off and police cars were everywhere. I told the cop at the barricade that I lived there—I wasn't even thinking about all the stuff we had in the car, guns, too—but he wouldn't let us go in. So I had my homie drop me off a couple of streets away and I walked back. Nobody stopped me until I got close to my house. A couple of cops told me I couldn't go any farther and I said, Hey, that's my house. That's where I live. There were t.v. cameras. I didn't even notice them until the cops stopped me. You can't go in there, one of the cops said. I asked him what was going on and he said my stepdad was holding my mother hostage. The police had come to arrest him for something, drugs probably, and he'd got my mother and was threatening to kill her. I asked if they'd let me go in and talk to him, but they wouldn't. Finally I went around to the back and just walked in. And there he was, with her, and she was already dead, and so was he. So I went outside—I walked out the front door and for a minute I thought they were going to shoot me. I think I wanted them to. I know I did. But they didn't. But, hey! I was on t.v.!

Business

I was in business. Weed, mostly. Cocaine, too.
Crack. Heroin. Whatever my customers wanted.
Sometimes I did business with some people from
another clique. I decided to have a party and I
invited these guys. Because I was in business and I
wanted something a little more than sometimes.

I have a sister.
Thinking of her now, how happy her face was when
everybody was arriving, I just...I can't say it. It's in
my chest. Thinking how she looked then makes me
happy now. When we were little she protected me.
From other kids. Also from our stepfather.
Or tried to.

There was money around.
And I, because I was in business.... In other words, I
was not being observant. I was not paying attention. I
did not see where people were going. I was making
money.

After awhile these guys
I'd invited came running up out of the basement.
Before I could ask what's-up they were out the door.
There were five of them. I went downstairs, and there
she was, my sister. And though she could not tell me,
I knew. Anyone would know. What had happened.

I got my homies and we went
to a house where I knew these guys chilled. Look at

my face. See how I am smiling? I cannot help it. There is nothing funny about any of this, anything I am telling you, but I cannot help smiling. That interests me.

Some of my homies surrounded the house. Eight of us went inside, by twos. People were there. They were having a party. I saw one of the guys. When I looked at him it was as though I was seeing him through a sheet of plastic. He seemed deformed. His edges did not hold, but melted into the air around him, then melted back. Nothing about him was still. His face was grainy, like wood, and thickened and thinned with its change of expression. We were separated by an immense distance which had nothing to do with where he stood and where I stood, but with the distorting lens that had set between us. Throughout my body I felt the sensation of needles stabbing me. I shot him until the magazine in my gun was empty. When I stopped shooting I saw that he had been holding a kid in front of him. As though the kid could deflect bullets. I did not see the kid until it stopped moving. I took another guy who had been at my party—the only other one I could find—and I and my homies took him to a house we knew was empty.

I remember how

the guy's skin smelled when we burned it. When the blood seeped. When it gushed. I took two days. Then I put him down like an animal I had no more use for. The sound he made then—like trying to breathe through water. As if the air was drowning him.

After that everything was different. The outlines of things were clearer, as though the distance between me and...whatever...had closed. My homies said I could not have done different. Shooting that guy would not have been enough. They knew me. But they looked at me as though I was different now.

I was.

From the time they raped my sister it was one of those situations where you have to do something and no matter what you do you are going to have to pay for it. I look at it as the time when I began to grow up, although I was already thirteen when all of that happened.

The Thrill of the Day

I got bored at school and decided
to chill with some white girls I knew
who give b.j. because they want to
save their virginity for when they
get married. But before anything
happened my pager went off so I
hopped on a bus to get across town
to where my homies were calling me.
      On the way I stopped at my cousin's
house to get a strap and then my
cousin and me and his damn dog which
he said was half wolf started walking
toward home. We were in Norteño
territory and soon, first two, then four,
then seven, then more were walking
behind us. They had sticks and
machetes and knives and bats.
      I turned and shot at them, but after
the first shot the gun was empty. I
told my cousin to turn the dog loose
on them but he said no, he didn't
want his dog to get hurt. Your dog
get hurt? I yelled. What about me?
I'm your cousin! But he wouldn't
let the dog loose even though I
kept yelling Do it! Do it! Do it!

Let go the damn dog! Finally I
took my cousin's gat and I ran in
one direction and my cousin and
his damn wolf-dog ran in another direction
and the Mexicans ran after me.
            I passed a guy I knew was a Crip
sitting on his porch. He had his guns
next to him and I yelled for him to
help me. I thought because our race was
the same and it was Mexicans
chasing me, he might help even if
he was a Crip, but he picked up his
guns and went inside.
            Then I got to a McDonald's and
went in. I could see the Norteños
at all the entrances, and at the windows.
I yelled to people in the restaurant
to call the police but nobody
did anything. When the Norteños
came inside I fired my gun into
the air until I used up all three
bullets. People were trying to get
under those little tiny tables
and kids were running all around, their
mothers were screaming at them, and I
was able to get into the bathroom.

I squatted on a toilet seat like
they do in movies so they couldn't
see my feet when they looked under the
door. But they found me and
beat on me with their sticks.
        "Fuck you, fuck you, fuck you!" I said.
        "You motherfucker, why did you shoot
 at us?"
        "Because I could!"
        And they beat on me and kicked me
even as I crawled under the sink
to get away from them.
        "Fuck you, fuck you, fuck you!" I said.
        And I was all crunched up like this, and
finally they left. All I got out
of it was a bruised elbow from when
I was trying to protect my head
when they were hitting me. I don't know
why they didn't kill me. If I was
them I would have killed me.
By the time I hooked up with my homies
all the excitement was over.

Why We're On This Earth

Guy I had a disagreement with says he's gonna snap my neck. Says he's gonna punch me in my temple. Go ahead, I tell him, and he goes into a move and I don't flinch. It shook him. He couldn't believe I was gonna let him kill me. He goes into another move like he's gonna hit me on the side of my head. I don't do a thing. What about your family, he asks. What about your mother. Don't you think she'll miss you. She'll cry for a couple of days, then she'll forget me, I say.

When I get out of the facility I'm gonna find somebody to kill me. I don't know where I'll find him, who it will be, but I'll know him when I find him. If he won't do it, I'll trick him into it. When I find him I'll know him and I'll know what he has to do and I'll tell him and if he refuses I'll make him do it, one way or the other. God put us on this earth to die. That's all. I would commit suicide but suicide's a sin and I don't want to go to Hell. I want to go to Heaven and so I'll find somebody to kill me and God will see that I'm not committing a sin. And then I'll be finished with this horrible life.

Guy I had the disagreement with—it made me laugh, him being all scared when I told him this. I'm just gonna do what Gods wants me to do. Guy needs to watch out for himself. He's the one who's scared.

Bloody Work

1.

Sometimes my ears will ring when I'm at the swimming pool. This sound reminds me of what I heard after my girlfriend was shot. My friend shot my girlfriend. She was on the phone and he shot her in the head. He was high, playing with a gun he said was empty. But I had loaded it and put it next to him on the couch. I loved her. He was my best friend. Afterward he wanted to put her in a dumpster. I said no. She was still alive.

Sometimes I'll look at something—a lamp, a tree—and it will start moving and it will become Kathy. I had loaded the gun and put it on my lap. I was high and Benny picked it up. I loved her. Benny shot her. Afterward he wanted to put her in a dumpster.

I shot her. Benny loved her. Afterward we put her in a dumpster.

I loved her. I shot her. Her parents found her in a dumpster. She was still alive.

2.

I needed money and I went with a friend to rob

a store. We were inside when a man walked in. He wouldn't leave. My friend was saying "Do it!" but I didn't want any witnesses. I was thinking of the store clerk. It didn't occur to me to shoot the store clerk too. Then I got angry and I went up to the man who had walked in and I shot him three times in the face. He was still alive and my friend shot him again. Then we ran. We didn't even take any money.

I went to another friend's house. She was watching t.v. She was upset. Some boys had just killed her uncle. There was a picture of her uncle on t.v. It was the man we shot. "I hope they get those kids," I said.

3.

I didn't get caught. They didn't do anything to me about my girlfriend. I've done other things I didn't get caught for. Once I shot somebody in a drive-by. I have done some bloody work.

If I'm in a fight and the other kid has beaten me up, I will look for him, that night, or the next, or soon. If I have a gun I will come up behind him and put the gun to his head as a warning. If I do not have a gun, I will come up behind him with a baseball bat and I will hit him in the head with it. I will hit him until he stops moving. I go crazy when I get mad.

4.

Someday somebody will kill me. I should die for the things I've done.

Perpetrator

She was my best friend and when she asked me to do those things I did them. She said it was no big deal and she did them too and so I did too. After, James wanted to touch me there and I said no and Susan said it was no big deal again but I still said no and neither she nor James insisted. She went to sleep in the bed with him and I slept on the floor away from them but where I could hear if James got out of bed because my sister was in another bedroom and I needed to know if James was going in there. Eventually, though, not on that first night but on another, he did do things with my sister.

At first there was another girl, another friend of Susan's, and Susan told her first that it was no big deal to do what James wanted and Susan did it herself to show us that it was no big deal, and then this other girl did it and then because she did I did, because I loved Susan. I stopped loving her forever after I found out James was doing things with my sister.

When I told my mother about James she did not believe me. Neither did the counselor at my school, nor the principal, Mr. Johnson. They did not believe me because my sister would not admit that what I said was true. But then my sister told our mother that our father was doing things to her. I did not believe her but my mother did and our father went to jail.

I did not like my sister then. In fact I hated her.

I hated her because she did not back me up when she was supposed to, but then later she told on our father. Before that, when James was trying to do stuff to her, I tried not to let him. I did not win over him but I did try and when she would not back me up after I had tried so hard I began to hate her. She said she did not want to hurt Susan because Susan said she would be an orphan if James went to jail, and that was why she did not help me, although she sent our father to jail. I cannot say how much I hated her. I hated her so much I tried to kill her with a knife. After that she began feeling bad about putting our father in jail and for a while I didn't hate her as much.

But then she told some people that I had done something to a little kid I was babysitting. It was Susan again. Susan and I were babysitting together when we did it. I don't know why we did it. As soon as we saw it was hurting him we stopped. I made Susan stop. Even so, people started calling me names and I started hating my sister again. She didn't say anything about Susan, only me.

It was after James got sent to jail that my sister died. She did it with the knife. It was horrible, how we found her. I think it was because once Susan was an orphan she had to go live someplace else and we weren't allowed to see her or talk to her. And, of course, what she did to our father. So now she's gone and our father's gone and Susan's gone and it's just my mother and me.

Adventures with My Mom

One night my mom came home drunk and my dad got in her face, so she went in the kitchen and got a knife and chased him all around the house with it. Finally he ran into the bathroom and locked the door so she couldn't get at him. I was crying for her not to kill him, and after he locked himself in the bathroom she turned and said she'd kill me instead, so I ran into my bedroom and climbed out the window and hid in some trees. It took my dad two hours to find me. When he did, he said "Come on, we're going to the store." We went to the S&G Market and my dad bought a six-pack and opened a can and drank it. He said, "I'm tired of her shit."

I didn't see her much after they got divorced, but after I got kicked out of school my dad decided she could raise me. We went to Jonesville, Ohio where she was living. The way she ended up there was she was hitchhiking and a guy picked her up and drove her to Jonesville. He fixed her up with an apartment but she drank up the money he gave her and then she didn't have any money to stay there and she moved to a cheaper place.

When we got to Jonesville she wasn't getting any money from him anymore because he had left her for someone else. We talked with her awhile and then I told my dad I wanted to stay in a hotel. The stairs to my mom's apartment smelled like dog piss and there were cockroaches everywhere. My dad had forty dollars. I had stolen a twenty-dollar bill out of his wallet when we stopped for lunch on the way to Jonesville but he didn't know it. He paid for the hotel with plastic. We ate dinner in the dining room, then watched t.v. until one or two in the morning. When we got up we ate breakfast and then he drove me to Mom's apartment. He said it was going to be hard for him to leave me, and he gave me some money. In the end, I had all his money but he still had his plastic.

She had a new boyfriend, Jan. He used to go to the blood center every two weeks and get twenty dollars. You weren't supposed to go more than every eight but he used fake IDs. So every two weeks we would get shit-faced with all the Bud we could drink at a place called Tony's. I could get in because I was accompanied by someone over twenty-one. Jan was like a dad to me. He took care of me, put Mom's ass in detox, all of that.

My mom had gotten knocked up by a guy named Harold who lived in our building. He dumped her and started going with somebody else, but then broke up with her because she was prostituting. One night he came upstairs and wanted to come in, but Mom told him she was going to beat his head in with a baseball bat if he tried, so he threw a brick through our window.

We got evicted lots of times but we always came back. When we got evicted we would go to a roach motel. The first time, I found some blank checks that

Harold had lost. We knew he had two thousand dollars in the bank because he had bragged to us about it when he was drunk one time. Mom told me to sign Harold's name to a check so we could get a motel room and buy some whiskey. Jan came with us, but Mom and him got into an argument about her drinking so much in front of me and she kicked him out and told him to take his sober ass back to his own place. I felt bad for Jan because he was just trying to take care of her and me and she goes and pulls this shit.

The only thing I remember about that motel we were at that first time was getting Cokes out of the machine to mix with the Johnny Walker we got at the corner liquor store for nine dollars and sixty-four cents. I remember how much it cost because my mom was drunk and I kept the change from the twenty-dollar bill she gave me outside the store. All we did that night was get drunk and watch an old movie on t.v. until we passed out. In the morning, we stole the t.v. and pawned it for twenty dollars. That was what we did every time we were evicted—we checked into a cheap motel and stole the t.v. and took it to a pawn shop. Sometimes the motel was only ten dollars and we would get twenty for the t.v.

I was with my mom only three months. In those three months I saw everything. I saw men put money in her cunt and in her mouth. I saw her with two men at one time, and once with three men, one after another. I saw her naked-dance in a roomful of men, and one time in front of just me. She tried to sell me into prostitution. I was beaten up and raped by a guy who sold drugs to the junkies in our neighborhood. Here's how that happened.

I was walking to the market to get some chips and a guy asked me if I wanted to make twenty dollars. I had seen him around, though I had never talked to him. I said sure and got in his car. We drove around and then he stopped and told me to take a duffel bag up to this house and ask for Harry. I went up to the door and knocked but nobody came, so I went back to the car. The guy said he'd take me back to my place, but instead we went to this place that he said was his apartment. He told me to come in and he'd take me home in a minute. Inside, he mixed me a glass of gin and tonic. I had never had gin before, but it tasted good and I drank it all down. Soon I was so drunk I couldn't stand up. Before I knew it he was pulling my pants down. When I tried to get up, he punched me and knocked me down. Then he punched me again and I stopped fighting. I felt pain in my groin and stomach and my ass burned like somebody was holding a blowtorch to it. When he was done, he went into the bathroom. I could hear the shower beating in the tub. I was in so much pain I couldn't move, I just lay there on the floor. When he came out of the bathroom he was naked and he grabbed my hair and made me suck him until he came in my mouth. When I spat it out he beat me up again. Then he pulled on his pants, threw a twenty-dollar bill at me, and told me to find my own way home.

I walked around, not really knowing where I was going, until a cop stopped me and asked me what was wrong. I told him what had happened and he took me to a hospital. By the time we got there my pants were soaked with blood and a nurse gave me a shot. After that I don't know what happened until I woke up lying on my stomach on a bed in the hospital.

While I was being raped my mom was killing herself. It was Jan who found her. She had taken some pills and washed them down with Johnny Walker. She killed the baby that was inside her, too. It was Jan who called my dad and got me out of the hospital and put me on a plane back to him. I never saw my mom again after I got in that guy's car and I never saw Jan again after he put me on the plane.

I would have to say that in the end none of it mattered except that I was less complete than I was when I came into this world. Although, of course, I have no memory of that particular day.

Nothing's Changed

When he was finished he went to sleep
as though it meant nothing to him.
As though he did this every day of his life.
I got out of the back of the truck and
went around to the cabin and sat in there.
The gun was in the glove box and I took it
and put it in my pocket. If I'd had it
before, I would have killed him. I sat up
all night in the front of the truck and waited
for him to come up and try to mess with me again.
But he just snored away.
Think of the confidence he had to sleep like that
after what he'd just done to me. He knew me
in more ways than one, that's for sure.
                    I kept the gun.
I went to the police and they returned me
to my parents and I left again the next day.
Once, on the street, this old guy came up to me
and offered me some money. I pulled out my
gun and he backed off damn quick. His fat
little fingers were twisting and quivering
like blind worms come up out of the ground
after a rain, looking for they don't know what.
That gun scared him. It should have.
                    All in all it hasn't
affected my life. I do what I did before

it happened. Nothing's changed. I gay-bash
but I gay-bashed before that happened, too.
I'd like to kill them all.

I didn't snitch on him
because I was afraid. I admit it. My friend
James got killed because he snitched. The guy
got out and got his friends and they came and
found James and they killed him. Skinheads.
I saw it.

Nothing's changed except
I always have a gun now. I used to keep a
gun in my pocket before, too, but not
every day like I do now. So
nothing's changed.

Worlds Not My Own

One of the kids told me that Brien had broken his window. Mike went to check on him while I opened the blood-spill kit, put on gloves, gown, boots, started for Brien's room. Halfway there, Mike met me, said blood was everywhere. I stopped my progress, asked Mike to fasten the gown's ties behind me, it was flapping between my legs. (Time, time—everything takes forever. But this is the age of AIDS, and the boy had been a prostitute.)

Brien was sitting on his bed, his back against the far wall. His left arm was extended—there were fresh cuts but it had stopped bleeding. His right hand was pressed against the side of his neck. I thought he may have cut his neck or stabbed himself and was trying now to stanch the flow of blood. There was blood on his right hand but it was dry—it must have come from his punching the window. The right side of his head and torso were in shadow. Maybe two seconds had passed since I opened the door to his room. I was standing at its threshhold. I asked what was wrong, then stepped into the room.

He had a large shard of glass in his right hand and was holding it against his neck. When I saw it I drew back. I said, "Come on, Brien. Give it to me." He was terribly frightened. He was nearly unconscious with fright. Suns burned dimly in his pale eyes. I felt my balance shift. In his gray eyes I saw worlds not my own.

He made a quick downward motion with his hand and I heard something tear. Before I could move, he replaced the glass against his neck. I saw no fresh blood. Then—I don't know why; I could think of nothing else to do—I grasped his other hand and pressed it gently. As though he had been waiting for this specific signal, he threw the glass down on his bed and Mike came in and picked it up. I looked at Brien's neck where he had stroked the glass across it. It was raw but was not bleeding.

For a moment after Mike took Brien out of his room I sat on his bed, pulling myself out of his eyes, away from the planets orbiting his fear. For a moment. Two...

What Keeps Us Going

All the clucks was dying down in Everett so I
went up to Marysville to try to sell. I was with
three of my home boys. But after a while nothing
was happening so I came back home. I left my
home boys up there. And while I was gone they
got into some sort of problem with Big T's little
brother, and one of them shot him. Killed him,
yeh. After that, T would try to shoot me when
he saw me on the street, or he would try to punk
me. You know, he'd stop his car and talk shit
and I'd just say "Whatever" and keep on walkin'.
Or he'd be selling on my corner and he'd
have his home boys there so I couldn't do nothin'
about it. I was about eleven then, yeh.
He was about sixteen.

Finally I heard that he kept
a lot of money hidden in his house. So me and
my home boys watched the house until we were
sure nobody was there and then we busted in.
We wrecked that place, looking for the money.
I even went into the little girl's room and tore
her mattress up looking for it. Nah, she wasn't
there. But T's mother was. We thought the
house was empty but T's mother was laying
in her bed. I guess she was too scared to come
out, she was just waiting for us. We didn't do

nothin' to her, just tied her up and put tape on
her mouth. We got six dollars from her, and that
was all we got. But we wrecked his house, and
even though we were wearing our hats pulled
down over our faces he knew who did it.
That was two years ago when I was thirteen.
Couple of weeks ago I heard
he shot my brother. Killed him, yeh. So, now....
It never ends. It's what keeps us going.

R.I.P. Li'l Homie

Li'l homie come up to me and say
he want me to shoot him. Sure, I say,
where you want it? In the knee or the arm?
In the ear? In between those two big wolf
teeth you got in the front of your mouth?
Where you want it? I'm jokin' him, you see.
Clownin' him. He say no, he want me
to kill him. He ain't jokin'.
I see he ain't. I say, Li'l homie,
I can't kill you, you my li'l homie.
He shake his head, he say, I need to die,
I can't take this life no more.
Li'l homie, I can't, I say. I love you,
I can't kill you. He look at me then
for a long time, then he walk away.

He gets himself a rifle and he goes to
Enemyland. To the land of our enemies.
That's only a couple blocks from here.
Four blocks. And he hists himself up on
this store building that's got this flat
roof, and he plinks himself some li'l children.
Li'l enemy children. Five, six, seven years old.
Enemy children. And he come back to the
clubhouse and he say, You know that dude
on the t.v. who plink those li'l kids?

That me.
Other homies laughin' 'cause they don't
believe him, but I ain't laughin', 'cause
I know he ain't lyin'. I see in the way he says,
he ain't lyin'. Plus there's the thing before,
when he asked me to shoot him.
Homie, I say, 'cause he ain't li'l no more. Homie,
they just kids. Li'l children. What they do to you?
They enemy, he say, size don't matter.
Size matter, I say.
We starin' at each other in the eyes now,
neither of us backin' down. The others, they
quiet, they not sayin' anything, they watchin'
but they scared. They never seen li'l homie
like this. You all go on out of here, I say.
And they go out.
You gonna wreck us, ain't you? I say.
Homie nods his head yeh.
Why you wanna do that? You spose to
love your homies. He don't say nothin',
but this big tear starts comin' out his eye
at the corner by his nose. He don't wipe
it away nor nothin'. Do you hate us? I say.
No, he say, almost as though they ain't
no tear on his face.

Why you do this, I say. You know this
gonna come back on us. How we
explain killin' li'l kids?
Kill me, he say. And I say, That what
this all about, ain't it?
He nod his head again yeh, but he don't
say nothin'. He cryin' out both eyes now.
I can't kill you, homie. I love you
even you don't love us no more, I say.
I'll do it again, he say. He cryin' in
his voice now, he can't hide it no more.
But I know he mean what he say. He'll
do it no matter how much it hurt
him or anybody.
Homie, I say, but I can't say no more
'cause I be cryin' too.
      Please, he say.
      Why, homie? Why?
      I can't take livin' no more.
      Why, homie? What be so hard on
you? What make you special?
      Nothin', he say. I'm just me.
He laugh then, and I think maybe it over,
maybe he be li'l homie again. But then
he take out this gun and he say,
Send me out with love.

Homie...
And he put the front of the gun in his
mouth and he pull that trigger before
I could do a thing. And that how
he went out. And I wish to God
I done what he asked me, 'cause
he went out alone and I could have
sent him with love.
Li'l homie. R.I.P.

In The World

All Air Is Finite

I knew a boy who killed a man by dropping a
rock off a bridge into the windshield of his
passing car. After two years the boy had convinced
himself that the rock had dropped itself.
                    The hardest story I ever heard,
though one that ever repeats itself, concerns
a boy who, diving a ship wreck at ninety feet
with his father, witnesses his father's getting
tangled in a murk of cables and cannot
extricate him. Ultimately his father sends
him to the surface—all air is finite, a son's
no less than a father's—to locate help
but of course the only help he can find is the
help that will bring up the body.
                    This is as far as the story goes.
But there are questions.
What would the boy have told himself?
Certainly he would recognize eventually that his
father, grasping the fact of his imminent death, had
saved his son by sending him off in search of
illusory help. And inevitably the boy would have
asked himself what more he could have done.
But would he have asked himself when exactly
did he know his father would die?
Was it when he left him? Was it during his ascent?
Or was it only on that sun-bright surface, that

more common world of foot motility and
unencumbered speech, that he understood at last
that all air is finite? Would the boy, after two years
or three of grief, have persuaded himself to
despise his father for dying as he committed
his son to live?
What did the boy do with his life?
Did he mutilate it with drugs? Did he end it
with a gun? Did he hide in a
monastery or a university? Did he marry,
beat his wife, murder his children?
                    The boy who dropped the rock
that dropped itself went to prison, served his
time, got out. I lost track of him, though
I heard stories, unverified.
The second boy got life.

Senator McCarthy and Atomic Waste

Following the end of World War II my father worked at Argonne National Laboratories on the edge of the Argonne National Forest outside of Chicago. One of the things his particular laboratory did was to separate usable uranium from its ore. Part of the process they employed involved baking the ore in a lead-lined oven.

One day Senator Joseph McCarthy came to inspect the laboratory. Senator McCarthy's star was rising then and he was looking for treasonous persons and acts of perfidy by which to boost it further. During his inspection, Senator McCarthy noted that the uranium ore weighed less when it came out of the baking oven than it did when it was placed inside. The laboratory manager explained that the loss of weight was owing to an anticipated chemical reaction between the ore and the lining of the oven.

Senator McCarthy was not to be deceived. He wondered aloud who in the laboratory might be selling the missing uranium to the Russians. He said he would return to re-inspect.

When Senator McCarthy returned, he noted that the uranium ore weighed more coming out of the oven than when it was placed inside. The engineers knew that this was owing to the chemical reaction between the ore and the new brick lining of the oven. But they said nothing and waited for the senator's reaction. Their anxiety was needless, for Senator McCarthy was content.

Around this time, someone in my father's laboratory began to wonder what was being done with the radioactive waste the laboratory was producing. Someone asked the engineers and finally one of them admitted that he had been filling Mason jars with it, then burying the jars in the forest. He had not mapped the places where he had buried the jars.

My father told this to me.

One Thousand Meters From Ground Zero

I knew a man who, as a corporal in the Army, participated in the second test of a thermonuclear device conducted in the United States. This was made with what we now call a "dirty" bomb: its explosion would contaminate particulate matter and cast it outward through the air.

My acquaintance was one thousand meters from ground zero in a Sherman tank with two other soldiers. When the bomb went off it threw a flash of intense light. My acquaintance, one hand over his eyes, the other grasping his rifle, could see the bones of the hand that covered his face, could see the metal (but not the wood) of the rifle the other skeletal hand held, could see the steel of the floor of the tank through his hands of light and bone.

When, after the light, the wind came, it picked the tank up and threw it down on its side and scraped it across the sand of the desert for eight hundred meters. When the wind passed, my acquaintance and the two other soldiers climbed out of the tank through its hatch. They were blind. They could not find their weapons. My acquaintance remembered that he was supposed to locate his weapon but he was unable to do this. He did not know what else to do so he sat down by the tank. His mind, he told me, was a jumble of fragments. It was disassociating at a mile a second, faster even than that.

It seemed unable to fix on a single image but would jump to the next before making sense of the first. It could not find a context for anything. My acquaintance told me that if the Army thought its soldiers could resume battle immediately following a nuclear blast it needed to think again. His sight returned after he had been sitting beside the tank for what he guessed to be forty-five minutes.

He said that every year he went to an Army hospital where the doctors took a sample of his spinal fluid. So far, he said, he was fine. He was middle-aged now. He had two children who were normal, though very short. He put his hand, palm flat, about eighteen inches from the floor. Then he laughed. He was only kidding; both of his children were normal, he said.

When I met him he was a lieutenant colonel. When he was a corporal he was in a Sherman tank one thousand meters from ground zero because his father had ordered him there. His father was the commanding general of the post on which the bomb test was run. When he, my acquaintance, told me this, he grinned. In his grin were many things, none of which could be easily defined.

Fourteen Years

In the fourteen years since I'd last seen her
much bad had happened. These things:
her brother Mike's madness, then suicide;
her father's heart twisting, twisting,
rending at last on the anniversary of
his son's death; her mother's simplifying,
simplifying, until finally she was a girl again,
living with her own mother on share-
cropped land back between the Great and
the greater wars; her husband's
unemployment, his drinking
until he beat her badly enough to—
well, cracked pelvis, cheek bone, broken
teeth—that's enough for a short list.
                    She feared the lithium shuffle—
shoulders slumped as though collapsed on
a clothes hanger; chin dropped on the chest as
though in sleep or under the yoke;
hands open, dangling, incapable;
feet sliding forward in turn, each finding
its stability before its companion began its
move to catch up.
She had seen Mike when he was crazy. Well,
now she was crazy and submitted herself to
the institution. In six months her husband
got her children, met a woman, began the

divorce, and she, my old lover, my first old
lover, began an affair with one of her keepers.
"We made love a lot. It was what I needed."
The man was decent and for several months
after she left the hospital they continued to
make love until he married someone else.

          "In less than two years
I lost all the men in my life." Except when
she saw her children she used Friday and
Saturday nights to pick up men. So far she
hadn't got sick and she hadn't got hurt.
Although "One man, when I started to get
out of the car, said 'You touch that door
handle and I'll break your fucking arm.' He
was really angry at his ex-wife. I can't have
friends," she said. "What I have on Friday
or Saturday is all I can have."
With her fingertips she brushed at
her left cheek. As she told me her life since
me, her fingers went to her face.
Again, then again.
It was fourteen years more before I understood
she was tracing the memory of a river
tears had cut.

        What enraged her now

was thinking about her ex-husband's wealth,
his comfort, for with his new wife he had
grown rich. It wasn't fair that he and his wife
should have it all, and she, my old love,
nothing. And in that I heard again the girl I'd
known, and felt again my fear of her. And,
swelling with desire, knew again that she
was not good for me.
At love, she was, uncannily, as I remembered.
Her flesh rose to meet my hand, my hand
moved to place itself just...so. Our bodies
have their own memories. After, she
laughed, "Well, I got mine."

Palm Desert

The rear of the house looks out over
an L-shaped pond. There are no fish in
the pond. No snails. No algae. No
insects haunt its surface. (But
there must be insects. My hostess says
she's seen bats at dusk. They frightened her
neighbor.) The pond is lined with concrete.
Its water reflects the blue blue sky.
A pair of egrets perch in a palm
tree overlooking the pond, or among
the shrubs of an artificial
island built at the bend of the
artificial pond. The egrets are
real. When they fly they are white and
angular against the flat blue sky.
The palm tree is probably real.

Poolside, a cast-iron frog squats
beside a cast-iron turtle. Each
is one foot long, painted green. In the
house are three bathrooms. The faucets and
handles are brass, as are the knobs on
the doors leading out into the sun.
They are polished yellow as gold.

In the house is a real tree,

but the tulips are fake. There are both
real and artificial roses.
Other trees that are fake. Real
elephant ears but a fake bird
in a fake nest. A fake cactus
in fake blossom. Real morning
glory. In the kitchen a fake
ficus. "I used to have a ficus but
it made a terrible mess," says my
hostess. There are flowers whose
real-life counterparts I cannot
imagine living in a real world.

Near the kitchen is a girl doll on
a swing seat. The doll is about two
feet long. It has red hair. In the
living room is a larger girl doll.
It too has red hair. This one is
seated on a bench, like a park bench,
but smaller. This doll is barefoot. Its
patent leather shoes and little
lace-topped socks lie beside it on the
bench. My hostess' hair is red. Inch by
inch she relinquishes her life to the
inanimate.

*

But in her bedroom are other dolls,
none with red hair. Two small ones lay side
by side in a wooden cradle. Half
a dozen others occupy a
stuffed chair. Three are tiny animals. Cows.
Two are Raggedy Anns. One is blond.
All, including the cows, are dressed as
little girls, eight, nine, ten years old.

Photographs of my hostess' sons
are everywhere. In the photographs
her sons are eight, ten, fifteen, twenty.
There are photos of her parents,
fewer than the sons', but enough.

The bodies of the women I
meet in the town are hard, taut.
Their faces are determined.
Death may not be met here unless
one chooses to meet it. Yet
people die who do not wish to.
It is an anomaly.

Jerome Gold is the author of three novels, *The Negligence of Death*, *The Inquisitor*, and *The Prisoner's Son*; two collections of stories, *Of Great Spaces* and *Life at the End of Time*; and the collection of interviews, *Publishing Lives: Interviews with Independent Book Publishers in the Pacific Northwest and British Columbia*. He also contributed to and edited *Hurricanes*, a collection of letters and essays about the human experience of hurricanes. He has published poetry, essays and short stories in Left Bank, Chiron Review, Hawaii Review, Vietnam Generation, Fiction Review, Poets on the Line and other literary journals. In 1999 His novel *Sergeant Dickinson* will be published, and in 2000, *Obscure in the Shade of the Giants: Publishing Lives Volume II*.

For several years Mr. Gold has worked as a counselor in a prison for youth offenders, which experience informs *Prisoners*.